This book is dedicated to:

CONTENTS

- 4   Organize My Life
- 13   Organize This
- 28   Set (And Keep) Your Priorities in Life
- 48   Organize Your Thoughts
- 54   Organize Your Memories
- 58   Organize Your Health
- 76   Digital Organization
- 88   Organize Your Cleaning
- 102   Life Hacks for Organizing Your Space
- 120   Ways to Live with Less
- 134   Rich Plan for Organizing Your Finances

WELCOME

A few quick tips on how to make this Organization Planner personal:

- This should add value to your life, not stress. Make it fun, but make it yours.

- There is no right or wrong, no first place to start. Just open it and go! Start in the middle, start at the end, start on the first page. You can start and stop anywhere.

- Get creative, add washi tape, add tabs, add color, add notes.

- Look at you making history. This is a chronicle of exactly where you are at in this stage in life. You are putting together an organized history for yourself.

ORGANIZE MY LIFE

Get it out of your head and onto something: Write it down, text it, make a note, but most of all - make sure it is somewhere besides just in your head!

Make the best use of a schedule, even if it is just for your daily life.

A place for everything, and everything in its place. Don't leave your everyday items homeless.

Constantly evaluate the value an item brings to you. **Mo' Stuff, Mo' Problems.**

Dedicate a short span of time every day to staying organized (10-15 mins should do the trick!)

Have a set information center - this is where those pesky reminders, notes and to do's should wind up.

Be savage to areas that accumulate clutter.

Designate PRIORITIES. Start small. 3-5 priorities each day.

SIMPLIFY, SIMPLIFY, SIMPLIFY

Say No and move on. Don't clutter your schedule with unwanted, unnecessary engagements.

Plan for failure - so you can plan to take care of that too!

ORGANIZE MY LIFE

[   ]

[   ]

[   ]

ORGANIZE MY LIFE

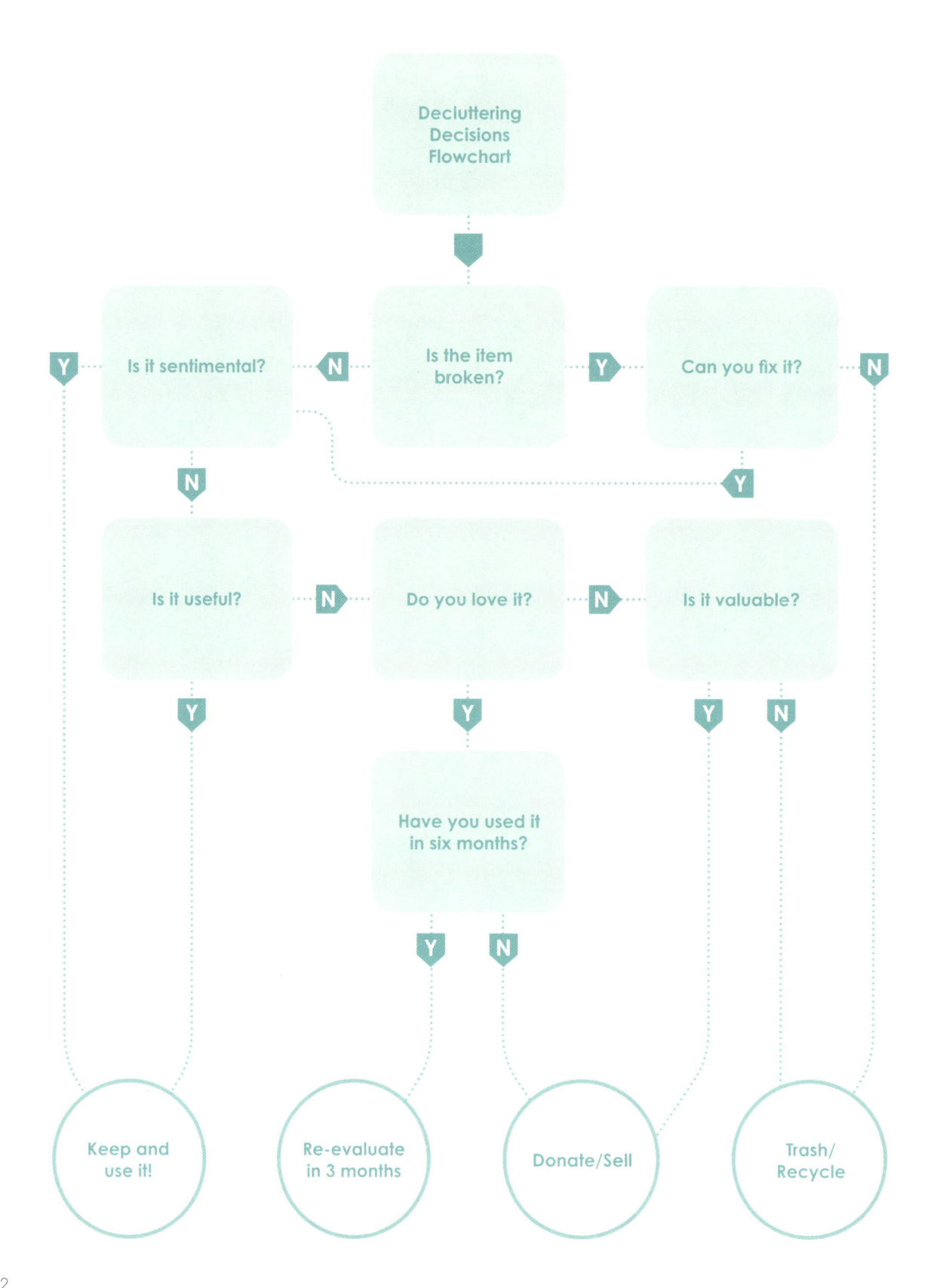

Decluttering Decisions Flowchart

```
                    Decluttering
                    Decisions
                    Flowchart
                         │
                         ▼
    ┌─────────────┐  N  ┌──────────┐  Y  ┌──────────────┐  N
  Y─┤Is it        ├◄────┤Is the    ├────►┤Can you fix it?├──┐
    │sentimental? │     │item      │     │              │  │
    └──────┬──────┘     │broken?   │     └──────┬───────┘  │
           │N           └──────────┘            │Y         │
           ▼                                    ▼          │
    ┌─────────────┐  N  ┌──────────┐  N  ┌──────────────┐  │
    │Is it useful?├────►│Do you    ├────►│Is it valuable?│ │
    │             │     │love it?  │     │              │  │
    └──────┬──────┘     └────┬─────┘     └───┬──────┬───┘  │
           │Y                │Y              │Y     │N     │
           │                 ▼               │      │      │
           │          ┌─────────────┐        │      │      │
           │          │Have you used│        │      │      │
           │          │it in six    │        │      │      │
           │          │months?      │        │      │      │
           │          └──┬───────┬──┘        │      │      │
           │             │Y      │N          │      │      │
           ▼             ▼       ▼           ▼      ▼      ▼
        (Keep and  (Re-evaluate  (Donate/Sell)    (Trash/Recycle)
         use it!)   in 3 months)
```

ORGANIZE THIS

Declutter these areas. Come on, be specific!

Jot down why these areas mean the most to you. This is your mantra!

- _____
- _____
- _____
- _____

- _____
- _____
- _____
- _____
- _____
- _____
- _____
- _____

- _____
- _____
- _____
- _____
- _____
- _____

Tip: Try drawing out the flow of each room so you can see your high touch points.

Carve out your day or week. Fill in the slices.

Make it fun and help yourself stay focused: Put your alerts on silent and turn on some music.

ORGANIZE THIS

SIMPLIFY THESE THINGS

Home

Health

Relationship

Activities

Projects

"We need much
less than we
think we need"
- MAYA ANGELOU

"

Your next great quote!

"

"Simple can be harder than complex: You have to work hard to get your thinking clean to make it simple. But it's worth it in the end because once you get there, you can move mountains."

– STEVE JOBS

ORGANIZED CELEBRATING

These are the most important holidays to me (rank them):

HOLIDAY NAME:　　　　　　　SPECIAL MEMORY FROM THAT HOLIDAY:

1
2
3
4
5

Prep for each holiday in advance:

HOLIDAY NAME:　　　　　PREP NEEDED:　　　　　　　FOOD OR GIFT TO BRING:

ORGANIZED GIFT GIVING

PERSON: GIFT IDEA:

Tip: Jot down gift ideas through the year as that person mentions things so your gifts can be specific and meaningful!

WISH LIST (hey it's OK to know what you'd like as a gift!)

"Simplicity is the essence of happiness."
- CEDRIC BLEDSOE

"Voluntary simplicity means going fewer places in one day rather than more, seeing less so i can see more, doing less so i can do more, acquiring less so i can have more."
— JON KABAT-ZINN

> "Whatever state I be in, therein I be content"
> – HELEN KELLER

DE-STRESS THESE AREAS OF MY LIFE

Get Rid Of This
-
-
-
-
-
-
-
-

Add That
-
-
-
-
-
-
-
-
-

Partake in This
-
-
-
-

Use That
-
-
-
-
-
-

SET (and keep) YOUR PRIORITIES IN LIFE

SET (AND KEEP) YOUR PRIORITIES IN LIFE

Your Goals In This Phase Of Life

Main
Goals

Secondary
Goals

Outlier
Goals

How I Get There

January

February

March

April

May

MY PRIMARY GOAL FOR THE YEAR IS...

June

July

August

September

October

November

December

SET (AND KEEP) YOUR PRIORITIES IN LIFE

DRAW IT OUT!

SET (AND KEEP) YOUR PRIORITIES IN LIFE

What's Important To Me

AND WHY...

-
-
-
-
-
-
-
-
-
-
-
-
-
-
-
-
-
-
-
-
-
-

SET (AND KEEP) YOUR PRIORITIES IN LIFE

Things I'm Passionate About

> "Passion is energy. Feel the power that comes from focusing on what excites you."
> —OPRAH WINFREY

SET (AND KEEP) YOUR PRIORITIES IN LIFE

"

Quotes that inspire me...

"

SET (AND KEEP) YOUR PRIORITIES IN LIFE

Organize Your Roadblocks To Focus On Your Priorities:

Blocker: _____ How to conquer: _____

Blocker: _____ How to conquer: _____

Blocker: _____ How to conquer: _____

Blocker: _____ How to conquer: _____

Blocker: _____ How to conquer: _____

What Inspires You?
Clip It, Rip It, Stick It Here:

SET (AND KEEP) YOUR PRIORITIES IN LIFE

SET (AND KEEP) YOUR PRIORITIES IN LIFE

SET (AND KEEP) YOUR PRIORITIES IN LIFE

Stay Curious
I WANT TO LEARN THESE **THINGS**

THING:

Why it brings value

When I plan to learn this

THING:

Why it brings value

When I plan to learn this

THING:

Why it brings value

When I plan to learn this

THING:

Why it brings value

When I plan to learn this

SET (AND KEEP) YOUR PRIORITIES IN LIFE

THING:

Why it brings value

When I plan to learn this

THING:

Why it brings value

When I plan to learn this

THING:

Why it brings value

When I plan to learn this

THING:

Why it brings value

When I plan to learn this

THING:

Why it brings value

When I plan to learn this

THING:

Why it brings value

When I plan to learn this

47

ORGANIZE YOUR THOUGHTS HERE

SET (AND KEEP) YOUR PRIORITIES IN LIFE

DATE:

DRAW IT OUT

SET (AND KEEP) YOUR PRIORITIES IN LIFE

SET (AND KEEP) YOUR PRIORITIES IN LIFE

DRAW IT OUT!

ORGANIZE YOUR MEMORIES

BE YOUR OWN STORYTELLER

BEST MEMORY EVER! _____
_____
_____

OMG remember this? _____
_____
_____

And that time when... _____
_____
_____

What would you want to read in your autobiography?

```
┌─────────────────────────────────────────────────┐
│                                                 │
│                                                 │
│                                                 │
│                                                 │
└─────────────────────────────────────────────────┘
```

In this Year _____ I am _____
_____
_____

In this Year _____ I am _____
_____
_____

In this Year _____ I am _____
_____
_____

TO DATE, MY BEST:

Trip

Kiss

Meal

Date

Experience

Teacher

Gift

Mistake

Moment

Joke

Discovery

Class

SET (AND KEEP) YOUR PRIORITIES IN LIFE

VENT IT OUT HERE

Go ahead. Write anything. It will always stay hidden.

organize YOUR HEALTH

ORGANIZE YOUR HEALTH

SLEEP

Sleep habits are best demonstrated in patterns. Be conscious about sleep!
After these two weeks, analyze and move on to a better sleep.

WEEK 1

	IN BED AT	WOKE UP AT	TOTAL HOURS
Sunday	_____	_____	_____
Monday	_____	_____	_____
Tuesday	_____	_____	_____
Wednesday	_____	_____	_____
Thursday	_____	_____	_____
Friday	_____	_____	_____
Saturday	_____	_____	_____

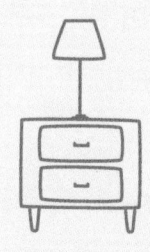

Have a nightstand? Keep it free of clutter. Put only the necessities and the things that bring calmness or things you love on your nightstand. If decor is junky or makes you see dust - away it goes!

ORGANIZE YOUR HEALTH

sweet dreams...

WEEK 2

	IN BED AT	WOKE UP AT	TOTAL HOURS
Sunday	_____	_____	_____
Monday	_____	_____	_____
Tuesday	_____	_____	_____
Wednesday	_____	_____	_____
Thursday	_____	_____	_____
Friday	_____	_____	_____
Saturday	_____	_____	_____

Flag this page and jot down your middle of the night worries so you can go back to sleep and not feel pressured to remember them.

ORGANIZE YOUR HEALTH

WATER

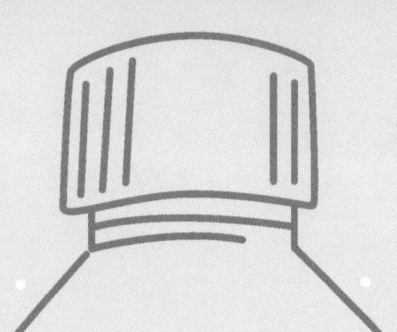

Recommended water intake is 90 - 125 oz per day.
Chart your intake daily and weekly.

WEEK 1 _____

WEEK 2 _____

WEEK 3 _____

WEEK 4 _____

WEEK 5 _____

WEEK 6 _____

WEEK 7 _____

WEEK 8 _____

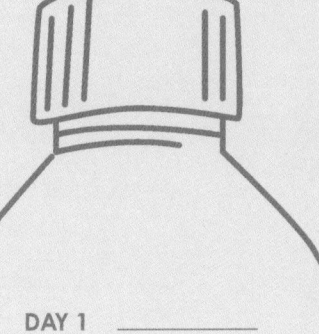

DAY 1 _____

DAY 2 _____

DAY 3 _____

DAY 4 _____

DAY 5 _____

DAY 6 _____

DAY 7 _____

ORGANIZE YOUR HEALTH

DAY 1 _____	DAY 1 _____
DAY 2 _____	DAY 2 _____
DAY 3 _____	DAY 3 _____
DAY 4 _____	DAY 4 _____
DAY 5 _____	DAY 5 _____
DAY 6 _____	DAY 6 _____
DAY 7 _____	DAY 7 _____

EATING HABITS

ORGANIZE YOUR MEAL PLANNING

	MON	TUE	WED
Breakfast			
Lunch			
Dinner			
Snack			

Ingredients I have:

_____

_____

_____

_____

_____

ORGANIZE YOUR HEALTH

THU	FRI	SAT	SUN

Ingredients I need:
_____
_____
_____
_____
_____

COLOR IT IN

De-stress here

69

THE GRATITUDE LOG

I'm thankful for:

_____

_____

_____

_____

_____

_____

_____

These people have changed my life:

PERSON: WHY:

"Gratitude unlocks all that's blocking us from really feeling truthful, really feeling authentic and vulnerable and happy."
- GABRIELLE BERNSTEIN

ORGANIZE
That Workout Plan

My goal for exercise is: _____

I'm committing to: _____

	DAY	ACTIVITY	DURATION
1	_____	_____	_____
2	_____	_____	_____
3	_____	_____	_____
4	_____	_____	_____
5	_____	_____	_____

MY MOVEMENT MANTRA IS:

DIGITAL ORGANIZATION

DIGITAL ORGANIZATION

GETTING RID OF DIGITAL CLUTTER

My Digital Clutter that Feels Overwhelming...

- [ ] _____
- [ ] _____
- [ ] _____
- [ ] _____
- [ ] _____
- [ ] _____
- [ ] _____
- [ ] _____
- [ ] _____
- [ ] _____
- [ ] _____
- [ ] _____

Check it off when you tackle it!

DIGITAL ORGANIZATION

Keep that inbox clear.
Archive is your friend.

Create a second account to use for fun info so it doesn't rule out work/school/events.

Make those new files now and then add to them. A cluttered desktop makes it impossible to find anything. Get an online drive to always have those files backed up.

Filter all incoming mail into set folders.

BEFORE AFTER

79

SOCIAL MEDIA CLUTTER

How I want to be intentional on Social Media:

Plan out some posts:

TITLE	THEME	DATE

Schedule your posts so you can set them and forget them.
Find programs like Later.com to set your instagram posts for anytime.

PHOTOS

PHOTOS

...and more photos

What to do if your phone's storage is full

CHECKLIST TO ORGANIZE PHOTOS:

DIGITAL ORGANIZATION

- [ ] Clear out unwanted pics
- [ ] Choose organization software
- [ ]
- [ ]
- [ ]
- [ ]
- [ ]
- [ ]
- [ ]
- [ ]
- [ ]
- [ ]
- [ ]
- [ ]
- [ ]
- [ ]
- [ ]
- [ ]

Tip: Don't forget about those burst photos - they take up a lot of space!

Organize those cords to keep your digital junk in order

Twist ties

Washi over toilet paper rolls to stuff long cords in

Use books to hide that ugly router

DIGITAL ORGANIZATION

Hair clip for small cords needing to stay looped

Over the door shoe rack to store bundles of cords

Butterfly clips to keep them on the table

DIGITAL ORGANIZATION

ORGANIZE YOUR CLEANING

ORGANIZE YOUR CLEANING

LIFE CLEANING CHALLENGE

Who needs a chore chart as an adult? Frankly... all of us.

Instructions: Pick one area of your house for that day (it can be as big as an entire room or as small as a single drawer) and make your own 10 day cleaning challenge.

DAY 1

DAY 2

DAY 3

DAY 4

DAY 5

DAY 6

DAY 7

DAY 8

DAY 9

DAY 10

Tip: Want it to feel clean? Always keep your counters clear of junk.

CLEAN ME WEEKLY
yes, weekly

ORGANIZE YOUR CLEANING

- [ ] Kitchen

Tip: Clean your microwave with vinegar on a sponge in less than 2 minutes.

- [ ] Bathroom

Tip: Keep an extra set of gloves, some vinegar, and a brush in each bathroom. You'll be more likely to clean on the spot if everything is there.

- [ ] Bedroom

Tip: Buy that extra set of sheets. So, if laundry is ignored for a few days, you still have sheets. (This is a big plus in life.)

- [ ] Dust

Tip: Use a fabric softener to wipe all your high dust areas, such as baseboards and shelves.

PRO TIPS

Know who has the best tips? Those who have done this!
Get the conversation going. Ask your favorite people!

Best Cleaning Tip from: _____

Best Cleaning Tip from: _____

Best Cleaning Tip from: _____

Best Cleaning Tip from: _____

Best Cleaning Tip from: _____

Cleaning Task List

_____

_____

_____

_____

_____

_____

_____

_____

_____

_____

_____

_____

_____

UpCycle your cleaning hacks:

Use a microfiber cloth cut in the size of your dust sweeper with edges sewn up to reduce waste and have a reusable mop!

Even better - use an older microfiber sock, just slide it right over the dust sweeper!

Take that same micro fiber cloth and secure it to a pair of tongs or a broom with a rubberband. Ah ha! A duster for hard to reach areas like shutters or blinds.

ORGANIZE YOUR CLEANING

CLEANING SCHEDULE
Daily, Weekly, Monthly, Whenever I get to it

DAILY	WEEKLY	MONTHLY

GUIDE TO STAINS

ORGANIZE YOUR CLEANING

IF YOU HAVE ONE OF THESE STAINS:	REMOVE IT WITH THIS:	IF YOU HAVE ONE OF THESE STAINS:	REMOVE IT WITH THIS:
Grass	Vinegar	Deodorant	Denim
Red Wine	White Wine	Make-up	Shaving Cream
Grease	Soda	Lipstick	Baby Wipe
Blood	Hydrogen Peroxide	Ink	Milk
Oil	White Chalk	Sweat	Lemon Juice
Coffee	Baking Soda		

My favorite stain-removing tip:
_____
_____
_____

Cleaning hacks everyone should know:

To remove dried, cakey food splatters in a microwave, heat up a bowl of water with half of a lemon for 3 minutes. Wipe clean with ease!

Pet hair, your hair, that fabulous blanket hair stuck places? Just use a dry squeegee everywhere and it easily collects the hair.

Let those dryer sheets go to work - run them over faucets to repel fingerprints.

Vacuum head all tangled with hair (not yours of course), use a seam ripper to get all those hairs cut right off and have the vac running at full capacity.

Wipe down your phone or tablet with a soft cloth - for example, a lens cloth. Avoid getting moisture in openings. No matter how tempting, refrain from using cleaning products.

Waxy or dirty ear buds? A little spritz of rubbing alcohol on a tooth brush makes for some fresh, clean (wax free) buds.

Machines that clean for you? Don't forget that they need cleaning too: Run your washing machine on the clean cycle with plenty of vinegar.

Put vinegar in your dishwasher at the highest temperature. (That small drain in the bottom needs some TLC too! Don't forget that's where food gets stuck!)

What works for me:

CLEANING SUPPLY CHECK LIST

- [ ] _____
- [ ] _____
- [ ] _____
- [ ] _____
- [ ] _____
- [ ] _____
- [ ] _____
- [ ] _____
- [ ] _____
- [ ] _____
- [ ] _____
- [ ] _____
- [ ] _____
- [ ] _____
- [ ] _____

Make my Own:
- [ ] _____
- [ ] _____
- [ ] _____
- [ ] _____
- [ ] _____
- [ ] _____

Make my Own:
- [ ] _____
- [ ] _____
- [ ] _____
- [ ] _____
- [ ] _____
- [ ] _____

ORGANIZE YOUR CLEANING

ORGANIZE YOUR CLEANING

LIFE HACKS
for
ORGANIZING
your
SPACE

LIFE HACKS FOR ORGANIZING YOUR SPACE

My space

When I'm here, I feel: _____

What Home Means to Me

15 Minute Organization Sprint

Mon - 15 mins at ____:____ to organize my: _____

Tues - 15 mins at ____:____ to organize my: _____

Wed - 15 mins at ____:____ to organize my: _____

Thurs - 15 mins at ____:____ to organize my: _____

Fri - 15 mins at ____:____ to organize my: _____

Sat - 15 mins at ____:____ to organize my: _____

Sun - I want to simply: _____

LIFE HACKS FOR ORGANIZING YOUR SPACE

My Own Organizational Tips that Work for Me:

- [ ]
- [ ]
- [ ]
- [ ]
- [ ]
- [ ]
- [ ]
- [ ]
- [ ]
- [ ]

> "It takes as much energy to wish as it does to plan."
> – ELEANOR ROOSEVELT

> "Clutter is nothing more than postponed decisions."
> – BARBARA HEMPHILL

Easy to Forget Spots that Need Some Organizing Love

LIFE HACKS FOR ORGANIZING YOUR SPACE

- [ ] Refrigerator
- [ ] Work Bag or Purse
- [ ] Make-up or Toiletry drawer
- [ ] Mail bin
- [ ] Shoe Stash
- [ ] Coat Closet
- [ ]
- [ ]
- [ ]
- [ ]

ORGANIZE YOUR CLOSET

I will arrange these:

I will sort these:

These always wind up on the floor:

Items I use the most:

Tip: Keep that top shelf organized with less used items.

Tip: Use up wall space and back of closet or cabinet doors.

Tip: Bulky clothes? Try rolling them and placing in a hanging shoe holder.

Tip: Keep bins available for easy purging: (Donate) (Trash) (Seasonal)

Tip: Keep leather purses looking nicer longer by hanging them.

Tip: Be strict about what clothes or shoes you absolutely love.

Tip: Matching hangers creates uniform space to easily navigate that closet.

LIFE HACKS FOR ORGANIZING YOUR SPACE

Keep track of those pesky stickies

Keep track of those pesky stickies

Keep track of those pesky stickies

Keep track of those pesky stickies

WAYS TO *Live With* LESS

MINIMALIST TIPS

FOR ANY LIFE STAGE

WAYS TO LIVE WITH LESS

ALL ABOUT BALANCE

Everything in my life, (example: my space, my relationships, my stuff),
must: (example: bring value to my life)

Now you try!

Everything in my life (my _____, _____, and _____) must:
_____

Everything in my life (my _____, _____, and _____) must:
_____

Everything in my life (my _____, _____, and _____) must:
_____

Everything in my life (my _____, _____, and _____) must:
_____

WAYS TO LIVE WITH LESS

less
is
more

"There are two ways to be rich: One is by acquiring much, and the other is by desiring little."

- JACKIE FRENCH KOLLER

Try The 7 Day Minimalist Challenge

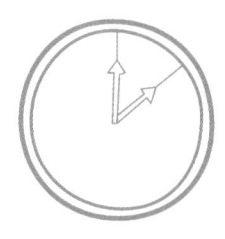

_____
_____
_____
_____

Day 1:
Take 10 minutes to stretch 3x's.

Comments:

Day 2:
Do not spend money for 24 hours.

Comments:

Day 3:
Clean all surfaces in your room.

Comments:

Day 4:
Clean your inbox.

Comments:

Day 5:
Practice mono-tasking.

Comments:

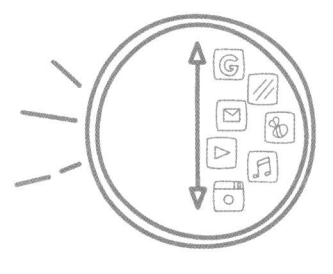

Day 6:
Media free after 6pm.

Comments:

Day 7:
Create a morning ritual.

Comments:

How I Want To Live With Less:

Start in this area:

I can swap _____ with _____
for quality over quantity:

Remove, but don't trash:

Stop feeling emotionally
attached about these:

Get rid of duplicates of these:

When this is all done, my goal is
to experience:

WAYS TO LIVE WITH LESS

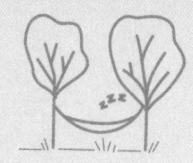

By Clearing Out My STUFF, I Will Feel...

"The consumption society has made us feel that happiness lies in having things, and has failed to teach us the happiness of not having things."

- ELISE BOULDING

Once you
need less,
you will
have more.

> "I'd rather have extra space
> and extra time than extra stuff."
>
> - FRANCINE JAY

RICH PLAN for Organizing your FINANCES

RICH PLAN FOR ORGANIZING YOUR FINANCES

Immediate Financial Goal:

Midterm Financial Goal:

Long-Term Financial Goal:

BALANCE THIS

WANTS | NEEDS

ORGANIZE YOUR FINANCIAL FILES

Need to sort your finances? List them out:

_____

_____

_____

_____

_____

_____

_____

WHOOPS!
Are You Forgetting To Budget These?

- [ ] Annual fees - if only some shopping Prime sites were free
- [ ] Pet expenses - they crop up out of nowhere
- [ ] Holiday expenses - gag, more gifts
- [ ]
- [ ]
- [ ]
- [ ]
- [ ]
- [ ]
- [ ]
- [ ]
- [ ]
- [ ]

Grow Those Funds

Instructions:
List out the areas of your budget you want to grow and start filling in the leaves.

Think your credit score is a judgy number?

Color to where your credit score is today (date _____).
Draw where you want it to be in 6 months.
Where you want it to be in 1 year.

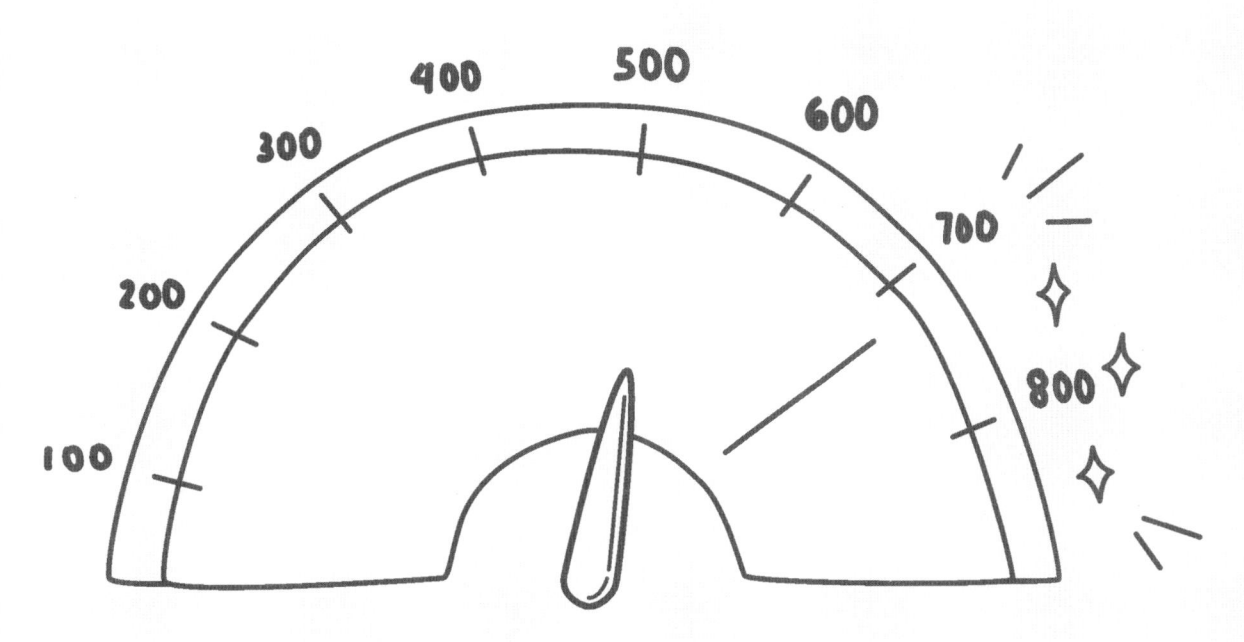

Credit scores are from 300-850
(anything over 720 is excellent so flag that 720 mark)

RICH PLAN FOR ORGANIZING YOUR FINANCES

My Organized Career

My dream job: _____
_____
_____

Other jobs that are similar: _____
_____
_____

Classes I'm taking that help me get there: _____
_____
_____

Contacts I know that are experts in this field: _____
_____
_____

Ways I plan to network: _____
_____
_____

How I'm setting myself up for success: _____
_____
_____

Career Goals

1 Month

3 Month

6 Month

1 Year

I Need To Make Room In My Budget For These Things:

- _____
- _____
- _____
- _____
- _____
- _____
- _____
- _____
- _____
- _____
- _____
- _____
- _____
- _____